Pony Problem

Do you love ponies? Be a Pony Pal!

PONY PALS

Pony Problem

Jeanne Betancourt

Illustrated by Richard Jones

A
LITTLE APPLE
PAPERBACK

SCHOLASTIC INC.

New York   Toronto   London   Auckland   Sydney
Mexico City   New Delhi   Hong Kong   Buenos Aires

Thank you to Natalie Deeb and Margaret Anne Rosenthal for sharing their love and deep understanding of ponies and horses.

ISBN 0-439-42626-X

12 11 10 9 8 7 6 5 4 3 2 1   3 4 5 6 7 8/0

Printed in the U.S.A.   40
First printing, January 2003

Contents

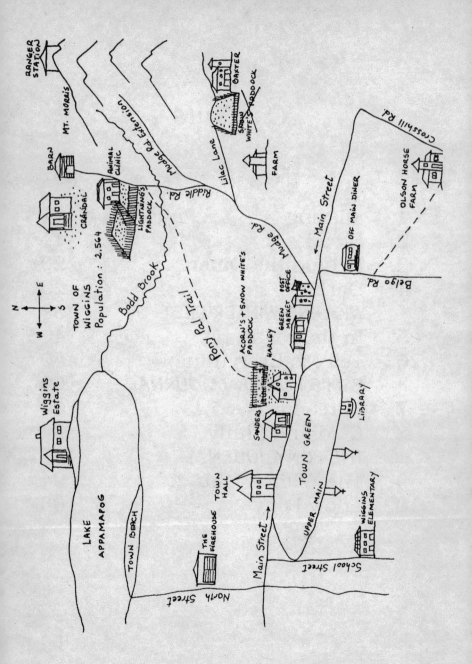

Pony Problem

Missing

*C*lank. *Clang.* The banging of the radiator woke Lulu Sanders. The air in her bedroom was hot and dry. Lulu felt thirsty. She threw off the comforter and went into the bathroom. As she drank a glass of water, she looked out the bathroom window. Her Welsh pony, Snow White, stood in the paddock near the open shed. It had been a snowy winter. Now a light dusting of new snow was falling.

Snow White in moonlight on a snowy night, thought Lulu. She repeated it out loud and added another line, "Everything is all right."

That's a poem, thought Lulu. She liked the way it rhymed and said it one more time.

> Snow White in the moonlight
> On a snowy night.
> Everything is all right.

Lulu was glad that it had snowed some more. The Wiggins Winter Fest was in a few days. There would be a lot of winter sports, so they needed snow. Lots of snow.

The Pony Pals were helping plan the festival. It would take place at Mr. Olson's Horse Farm. Mr. Olson's nephew, Charlie Chase, was helping too. Charlie lived in Wyoming and was an excellent western rider. He was going to demonstrate his western riding tricks at the Winter Fest.

Best of all, thought Lulu, Charlie is teaching me some western riding tricks.

When she was back under the covers, another thought popped into Lulu's head. She hadn't seen Snow White's stablemate, Acorn, in the paddock. Acorn was probably behind the shed, decided Lulu as she drifted back to sleep.

Two hours later, Acorn's owner, Anna, woke up and looked over at her clock radio. 5:58 A.M. Anna sat up and glanced out the window. It was still dark out, but she could see Snow White's coat glowing in the moonlight. Anna wanted to see her pony, Acorn, too. She went to the window and looked outside. First, Anna noticed that there was a light coat of newly fallen snow. Next, she saw that Acorn wasn't in the paddock. The only part of the paddock I can't see, thought Anna, is behind the shed. But the ponies only go there for shade in the summer.

Anna's heart pounded in her chest. Where was her pony?

She opened the window, leaned out, and looked to the left. Acorn wasn't in Lulu's grandmother's yard. She looked to the right. He wasn't behind the Green Market.

Anna pulled on her jeans and boots, put on a sweatshirt, and headed down the stairs. Her jacket and hat were hanging on a hook near the kitchen door. She rushed to the paddock and looked behind the shed just to be sure. Acorn wasn't there.

Snow White, she noticed, didn't move. She stayed in her spot near the shed.

"Where's Acorn?" Anna asked Snow White. Snow White didn't even turn toward her.

Anna ran out of the paddock and over to Lulu's. The key to the back door was on the porch behind the wood box. Anna unlocked the door and ran up the stairs to Lulu's room.

"Wake up," Anna whispered in Lulu's ear.

Lulu opened her eyes. "Anna!" she said with surprise.

"Acorn's gone," said Anna.

"Isn't he behind the shed?" asked Lulu.

"He never goes back there in the winter," said Anna.

Lulu nodded. She knew that. But she hadn't thought of it last night.

Lulu threw her legs over the side of the

bed and pulled off her pajama top. "My jeans are on the chair," she told Anna.

Anna handed Lulu her clothes.

"Someone must have stolen him," said Anna. "He wouldn't run away."

"He used to run away a lot," Lulu reminded her. "When you first got him."

"He only ran away because he was lonely then," said Anna. "He hasn't done that since Snow White moved in."

"He still might have jumped out of the paddock last night," said Lulu. "We don't *know* that he was stolen."

"You're right," agreed Anna.

Anna loved her Pony Pals — Pam and Lulu. She loved her family, too. And she loved to draw and paint. But above all, she loved Acorn.

Acorn was special and many people in Wiggins knew it. When the Yellow Tent Circus came to town, Acorn was in the clown act. He was in a Hollywood movie that was shot in Wiggins, and he was in a play at the library. Tears sprang to Anna's eyes.

"If Acorn is lost, I might not find him," she said. "If he's injured, he could . . . he could . . . " Anna wailed. "And what if he *is* stolen? What if I never see him again?"

Lulu put her hands on Anna's shoulders. "We'll find him," she said. "Remember, the first rule in an emergency is to stay calm."

Anna nodded. She took a deep breath.

"You write a note for my grandmother and your parents," instructed Lulu. "I'll pack for the search."

Anna stood at Lulu's desk and wrote the note. She was dyslexic, so reading and writing were difficult for her. She hoped that she wasn't making a lot of mistakes.

Lulu packed the binoculars and her camera. The binoculars could help them find Acorn. If he *was* stolen, they might need the camera to photograph evidence. Lulu packed the first aid kit, too, just in case Acorn was injured.

Mrs. Sanders
Acorn is mising. Lulu
and I are looking for
him. Plese tell my parints.
Anna

The girls left the note on the kitchen table and put on their gloves.

Pam Crandal's alarm went off. She was getting up an hour early to do her morning chores. Then she was going to go for an early morning ride to meet her Pony Pals at the Off Main Diner. After breakfast, the Pony Pals would ride to Olson's to work on the Wiggins Winter Fest. There was a lot to do, starting with the poster.

As Pam got out of bed she thought about how much she loved being a Pony Pal. Anna and Lulu were her best friends. Their ponies, Acorn and Snow White, were her friends, too. It's like we're six Pony Pals, she thought.

Pam's mother was a riding teacher. Pam had owned a pony for as long as she could remember. Her parents said she could ride before she could walk. But Pam loved all kinds of animals. She thought she might be a veterinarian some day, like her father. Even if she wasn't a veterinarian, she knew she'd always have lots of pets.

When Lulu opened the paddock gate, Snow White trotted over to her. She whinnied softly as if to say, "What are you doing out here so early?"

"Where's Acorn?" Lulu asked Snow White. "Where's your friend?"

Snow White turned and walked back to the shed.

"I wish Snow White could tell us what happened to Acorn," said Anna.

She glanced around the paddock. The newly fallen snow in the paddock was filled with pony tracks.

"First, we'll see if there are people tracks

in here," said Lulu as she moved a beam of light across the ground.

She stopped her light beam on a footprint and bent over it.

"I found tracks," she told Anna. "Someone was in the paddock."

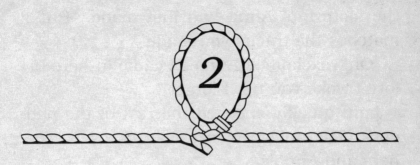

Blood

Anna and Lulu stared at the footprints in the snow.

"This looks like a kid's track," said Lulu.

"Maybe Mike and Tommy took Acorn!" exclaimed Anna. "It would be just like them to do something mean like that."

Tommy Rand and Mike Lacey were older boys who were always annoying the Pony Pals. Lulu thought Tommy's middle name should be "Trouble."

Lulu made a footprint next to the track she'd found. Hers was bigger. "It's too small to be theirs," she concluded. She looked at the footprints Anna had just made. "But it matches the tracks you made."

"Oh!" exclaimed Anna. "I came in here before I woke you up. I forgot."

Lulu quickly checked the rest of the paddock. The only people tracks she saw were hers and Anna's.

"Let's walk around the paddock on the outside," suggested Lulu.

The two girls followed the flashlight beam around the paddock.

I love being a Pony Pal, thought Lulu. And I love solving problems. But I'm scared that something awful has happened to Acorn.

Lulu didn't grow up in Wiggins like Anna and Pam. Her mother died when she was little. Her father was a naturalist who traveled all over the world to study wild animals. After Lulu's mother died, Lulu traveled with her dad. But when she was ten years old, Lulu's father said she had to live in one place for a while. That's when Lulu moved in with her grandmother Sanders on Main Street in Wiggins.

The two friends were halfway around the paddock. They hadn't found any people tracks or pony tracks.

"What if there aren't any tracks, Lulu?" asked Anna.

"There have to be," answered Lulu.

"Maybe Acorn was stolen *before* it snowed," suggested Anna.

"Good point," agreed Lulu. She was surprised she hadn't thought of that herself. Maybe I'm not such a great detective after all, thought Lulu. What if I'm not good enough to find Acorn?

Lulu and Anna continued around the outside of the paddock. Lulu passed the beam from the flashlight across the snow.

"There's one!" shouted Anna. She ran over to a hoofprint lit by the beam. "And here are some more."

"And no *foot*prints," said Lulu excitedly. "That's proof Acorn wasn't stolen."

Anna went over to the fence. "He jumped out here," she said.

Lulu followed the hoofprints with the flashlight beam. "And then he went toward Pony Pal Trail," she added.

"Come on," said Anna. "Let's follow his tracks."

"We should take Snow White to help us," suggested Lulu.

"Good idea," agreed Anna.

Pam went to the tack room to get food for the horses and ponies. A mouse skittered between her feet. She saw Fat Cat sitting in a corner.

"Fat Cat!" called Pam. "A mouse!"

A bored "meow" answered her.

"Aren't you going after that mouse?" asked Pam.

Fat Cat stretched out on the floor, put her chin on her front paws, and closed her eyes.

Pam knelt in front of the gray cat and stroked her fur. "What's wrong?" she asked.

"You love to chase mice. Why aren't you doing your job?"

Pam continued to stroke Fat Cat, but the gray cat didn't purr. Pam sat back on her heels and thought about Fat Cat.

She put her hand on Fat Cat's head and stayed focused on her. Suddenly, an image popped into Pam's head. In the image, Fat Cat was lying on a pile of saddle blankets on the shelf. She was purring. Pam looked up at the shelf. Someone had put toilet paper rolls on top of the blankets.

"You lost your favorite sleeping spot, Fat Cat," said Pam. "Is that why you're not chasing mice?"

Fat Cat didn't move.

Pam stood up and moved the toilet paper to the bottom shelf.

Pam glanced at her watch. It was time to feed the horses and ponies.

Lulu and Anna led Snow White along Pony Pal Trail.

"I wonder why Acorn ran away," said Anna.

"We might never know," said Lulu. "The important thing is to find him."

"I know," agreed Anna.

As the searchers followed Acorn's tracks, the sun rose. Lulu switched the flashlight off.

At the three birch trees, another trail entered Pony Pal Trail. This trail was on Ms. Wiggins's land. Ms. Wiggins was a friend of the Pony Pals. She lived in a big house and had a lot of great riding trails. Her driving pony, Beauty, loved to hang out with Acorn, Lightning, and Snow White.

"Maybe Acorn went to Ms. Wiggins's to see Beauty," said Anna.

Lulu didn't see any pony tracks in the snow on Ms. Wiggins's trail. But she saw more of Acorn's tracks ahead on Pony Pal Trail.

"Acorn stayed on Pony Pal Trail," she told Anna.

Snow White turned toward Ms. Wiggins's trail.

"Acorn didn't go that way," Lulu told her

pony. She put her hand under her pony's neck to pull her back to Pony Pal Trail. Lulu's fingers touched something sticky in Snow White's coat. She stooped to see what it was.

"Snow White has blood on her neck," Lulu called to Anna. "Come, look."

Anna came over and studied the bloody spot. "She must have cut herself," said Anna.

"On what?" asked Lulu. "There's nothing in the paddock for her to cut herself on."

Lulu was already taking the first aid kit out of her saddlebag. "Look at it. It's a pony bite," she said. "Acorn must have done it before he ran away."

"Acorn wouldn't bite Snow White," exclaimed Anna.

"He was the only other pony in the paddock," said Lulu as she opened the bottle of antiseptic.

Anna held Snow White's lead close while Lulu dabbed the antiseptic on the wound.

"Maybe Darling did it," said Anna.

Darling was Mr. Olson's newest purchase. She was a sweet gray Welsh two-year-old. Snow White loved Darling. The two Welsh ponies had played together the day before.

"We were all outside when Darling and Snow White were playing," said Lulu. "We would have noticed if they were fighting. Besides, it would have stopped bleeding by now."

Lulu felt angry at Acorn for hurting Snow White.

Acorn wouldn't bite Snow White for no reason, thought Anna. She wondered what Snow White did to make him bite her. And what did Snow White do to make Acorn run away?

Behind the Diner

After Pam fed the ponies in the barn, she walked to the paddock with a bucket of grain.

"Good morning, Lightning," she shouted to her pony.

Pam's Connemara pony trotted toward her. The school ponies — Splash and Daisy — followed.

A loud whinny also greeted Pam. It was coming from outside the paddock. Pam turned to see Acorn running toward her, too.

"Acorn!" shouted Pam. "What are you doing here?"

Pam looked around, but she didn't see Anna. She noticed that Acorn didn't have on a saddle.

"You came here by yourself!" exclaimed Pam. "Does Anna know you ran away?"

Pam opened the paddock gate. Acorn followed her into the paddock and stuck his head in the feed pail.

Pam laughed as she pushed his head away. "You are such a mischievous pony," she said.

"Anna, he's here," a voice shouted.

Pam saw Anna, Lulu, and Snow White running across the big field toward her.

Anna climbed over the fence and ran to her pony. "Acorn, you're safe!" she shouted joyfully as she hugged her pony.

Lulu tied Snow White to the fence and told Pam all about their search for Acorn. Meanwhile, Anna was petting Acorn all over.

"Acorn bit Snow White before he ran away," Lulu told Pam.

"Snow White bit Acorn, too!" said Anna. "Look!"

Anna showed Pam and Lulu a small bite on Acorn's rump.

"*That's* why he ran away," she added.

Acorn suddenly turned in Snow White's direction and whinnied. Snow White shied.

"We better put some antiseptic on this bite," said Pam.

"I have the first aid kit," said Lulu as she opened her saddlebag. She glared at Anna. "I needed it for Snow White."

Pam and Anna made a big fuss over Acorn. Snow White was still outside the paddock, tied to the fence. Lightning and the school ponies — Daisy and Splash — were eating. Acorn probably already gobbled down some grain, thought Lulu. He always wants to eat first.

Lulu went back in the paddock with the antiseptic. "I'll do it," Anna said as she took the antiseptic from Lulu.

"It's just a little cut from a branch," said Lulu. "It must have happened when he ran away."

"It's not little," said Anna. "Besides, Acorn

didn't go through a mess of scratchy bushes. We followed his tracks. They were all on open trail." She glared at Lulu. "I thought you were a detective."

Pam looked from Anna to Lulu. It's not just the ponies who are fighting, she thought.

"Can you guys help me with the rest of my chores?" asked Pam. "Then we can ride to the diner. Acorn can use Daisy's tack. Okay?"

"Sure," said Anna. "Why not?"

Anna and Lulu exchanged a glance. Anna thought Lulu looked angry. Lulu thought Anna looked mad.

"Okay with me," said Lulu. "But I can't stay at the diner too long. I'm working on western riding tricks with Charlie this morning."

"But we have to make fliers for the Winter Fest," said Anna. "That comes first."

"I know that," said Lulu. "That's why I want to get there early."

"Come on," said Pam. "Let's clean out the stalls."

"What am I supposed to do with Snow White?" asked Lulu. "Leave her here saddled up with no water or food?"

"You take care of Snow White," suggested Pam. "Anna and I will start on the stalls."

Anna followed Pam into the barn.

"Look," said Anna pointing to the doorway of the tack room. "Fat Cat caught a mouse."

Pam smiled to herself. Fat Cat was back to work. As Pam dropped the dead mouse in the basket, she heard a purr above her. Fat Cat lay on the saddle blankets. "Good work, Fat Cat," she said.

"Snow White made Acorn run away," Anna told Pam.

"Acorn bit Snow White, too," said Pam as she handed Anna a shovel.

Anna frowned at Pam. She hated when Pam wasn't on her side.

Outside, Lulu watched Acorn and Lightning running free around the paddock. Pam and Anna were in the barn. Lulu rested her head on Snow White's neck. "They were all friends before we even met them," she told Snow White. "You and me have to stick together, Snow White. Don't worry. I'll protect you from Acorn."

The Pony Pals rode single file to the diner. Pam followed Anna. Lulu and Snow White took up the rear. As they rode along, Acorn turned to look at Snow White. Lulu felt her pony tense up beneath her. Snow White is afraid of Acorn, she thought.

When the three riders reached the diner, Anna made an announcement. "Acorn and Snow White can't be at the hitching post together," she said. "Snow White might bite Acorn again."

"Don't worry," said Lulu. "I wouldn't let Snow White be next to Acorn, either. Acorn might hurt Snow White again."

Anna dismounted and tied Acorn to the hitching post next to Lightning.

"I'll tie Snow White to the fence behind the diner," said Lulu.

Anna's mother owned the diner, so the

Pony Pals could eat there whenever they wanted. Pam went behind the counter and poured them juice and milk. Lulu set the table. Anna put in an order for three blueberry pancake specials. When their breakfast was ready, the girls brought it to the booth.

As they ate, Pam noticed that Anna and Lulu were quiet.

"We have to figure out why Acorn ran away," said Pam.

Lulu slid out of the booth and stood up. "I have to check on Snow White," she announced. Lulu walked to the back window where she had a good view of Snow White. Her pony was standing alone at the fence with her head down. It made Lulu sad to see Snow White unhappy.

Lulu went back to the booth and sat down. "The next time we're here, Snow White should be at the hitching post with Lightning," she told Anna and Pam. "She thinks she's being punished."

"How do you know what she's thinking?"

asked Anna. "She's probably thinking, 'I wish I had bit Acorn harder.' "

"That's a stupid, mean thing to say," said Lulu.

Pam frowned at Anna.

Anna knew what she said was mean. But she felt like being mean.

"Sorry," Anna mumbled before she took another bite of pancake.

"By the next time we come to the diner, Acorn and Snow White will be friends again," said Pam.

"Maybe," said Lulu. "And maybe not."

I wish I could spend some time alone with Snow White or Acorn, thought Pam. Maybe I could figure out what's wrong with them. She wondered when she'd have a chance to do that.

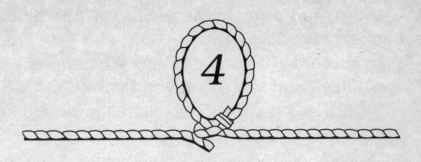

Darling

Charlie Chase ran down Mr. Olson's driveway to meet the Pony Pals. The girls dismounted and led their ponies the rest of the way to the barn.

Anna noticed that the only pony Charlie said hello to was Snow White.

He patted Snow White on the neck. "Darling's been waiting for you, Snow White," he told her.

"Snow White shouldn't be with Darling today," announced Anna. "Snow White is in a fighting mood. She might bite Darling."

"What?" asked Charlie.

"Acorn ran away because Snow White bit her," explained Anna.

Lulu scowled at Anna. "Snow White never, ever bites," she said. "And you know it."

"Well, she bit Acorn last night," protested Anna.

"Nobody but Acorn and Snow White know what happened last night," said Pam.

"Ponies are herding animals," said Charlie. "They like to stay together, even if they're fighting."

"We know that," said Pam. "You don't have to tell us."

"There has to be another reason for a pony to leave his herd," continued Charlie. "Especially for a male to leave a female."

"We know that, too," said Pam.

"So why did he leave?" Charlie asked Pam.

"That's what we have to find out," said Pam.

Acorn left because he's spoiled and does whatever he wants, thought Lulu.

Darling ran up to the paddock gate and whinnied hello to Snow White.

Snow White danced excitedly in place and whinnied back.

"Let them play together," said Charlie. "Snow White won't hurt Darling."

Lulu turned to Anna. "I told you so," she muttered.

The girls unsaddled their ponies, and Lulu put Snow White in the paddock with Darling. Acorn and Lightning shared the paddock next to them.

Next, the three girls and Charlie went to Mr. Olson's barn office.

There were a lot of art supplies on the desk and the computer was turned on. Four chairs were arranged around the desk.

"Pam, you sit in front of the computer so you can take notes," directed Charlie. "We'll start by making a list of what we're planning for the Winter Fest."

Charlie is so bossy, thought Pam.

"Oh, and here's some big news," exclaimed Charlie. "I have another event to add to the festival."

"What?" asked Lulu.

"A snowboarding demonstration," answered Charlie. "We'll have it on the hill behind the indoor ring."

"Who's going to snowboard?" asked Pam.

"Tommy Rand," answered Charlie. "He and Mike want to be part of the festival. Mike's going to help Ms. Wiggins give sleigh rides."

Charlie shouldn't have asked Tommy and Mike to be in the Winter Fest, thought Pam. He knows we don't like them.

"Tommy's teaching me how to snowboard," added Charlie. "It is so much fun. You guys should ask him to teach you."

Pam exchanged a glance with Lulu and Anna. They were thinking the same thing. They'd never ask Tommy Rand for *anything*.

"Okay," said Charlie. "Who has ideas for the flier?"

"I wrote a poem," said Lulu.

"I did some drawings," added Anna. She

reached into her jeans pocket and pulled out a folded piece of paper.

Charlie turned to Lulu. "You wrote a poem for the flier!" he exclaimed. "That's a great idea!"

"What is it?" asked Pam excitedly. "Tell us."

While Lulu recited her poem, Anna put her drawings back in her pocket. If Charlie and Pam don't care about my drawings, she thought, I won't even show them.

Pam typed Lulu's poem into the computer. Next, they answered the questions: Where? When? What? "Leave space for Anna's drawings," instructed Charlie. But no one asked to see them.

Pam printed out a few copies of the flier. Charlie handed one to Anna.

"While you do the drawings, Lulu and I can work on western riding tricks," Charlie said.

"I'll watch," said Pam.

Anna thought Pam was going to stay and watch her draw. She was surprised when

Pam followed Lulu and Charlie out of the room. I'd rather be alone, anyway, thought Anna.

When Lulu led Snow White out of the paddock, Acorn ran over to the fence. He nickered and curled his lip. Snow White looked at him and her ears went back.

"What are you going to do about Acorn and Snow White?" asked Charlie. "If they're fighting they can't stay in the same paddock."

"We're having a barn sleepover tonight," said Pam. "It'll be easy to separate them at my place."

But who gets to be in the paddock with Lightning? wondered Lulu. Snow White or Acorn? Which pony does Pam think is the bad pony?

Pam noticed Lulu's frown and knew what she was thinking. "I don't think Acorn is bad and I don't think Snow White is bad, either," she said.

Lulu's frown turned into a look of surprise. Sometimes the Pony Pals could guess one another's thoughts. But she was still amazed that Pam knew what she was thinking.

"We'll keep all our ponies in the barn tonight," added Pam. "Lightning can stay in a stall between Snow White and Acorn." And I'll put my sleeping bag between Lulu and Anna, thought Pam.

Anna did a drawing of a pony pulling a skier next to "skijoring" on the poster. Now, I'll do one of sledding, she thought. But after I finish my drawings Acorn and I are going home.

Half an hour later, Anna put away the art supplies and went to the indoor riding ring.

Lulu was practicing barrel racing. She turned Snow White right around one barrel, then left around the next.

"Look at Lulu," whispered Pam. "She's doing great."

"I didn't know Lulu could do western tricks so well," said Anna.

"She didn't, either," said Pam. "But she and Snow White are really good at it."

"I finished the drawings," said Anna.

"Good," said Pam. "When Lulu's done we'll scan them into the computer and print out the fliers." She looked at her watch. "We'll put them around town on our way home."

"I'm going home now," announced Anna.

"What about finishing the fliers?" asked Pam. "And hanging them up?"

"Charlie can help you," answered Anna. "I'm tired. I got up really early this morning."

A few minutes later Anna rode Acorn down the driveway.

"See you later," called Pam. "Rest up so we can stay up late tonight."

"Okay," Anna called back. But she didn't mean it. She leaned over and patted Acorn's neck. "Don't worry," she promised. "Snow White won't bother you anymore."

When Pam went back to the ring, Charlie was practicing his best trick. He was standing on Snow White's back while she ran around the ring.

When he finished, Lulu gave Snow White water.

Charlie looked around. "Is Anna still drawing?" he asked Pam.

Pam shook her head. "She went home."

"She didn't say good-bye," complained Lulu. "Was Acorn being bad?"

Pam shook her head. "Anna's tired. But she'll come tonight."

"It's good for Acorn to be alone for a little while," said Charlie. "He'll feel safer and so will Snow White."

"Maybe," said Pam. She kicked the dirt. She hated it when Charlie acted like he knew more about ponies than she did.

WIGGINS WINTER FEST

Winter can be cold and dreary
Making folks feel sad and weary.

There'll be snowy sports for all of you
Skiing, sledding, and sleigh rides, too.

At Olson's Farm there's winter fun
We'll all be smiling when we're done.

Come to the WIGGINS WINTER FEST!
It's going to be the very best!

WHEN? 12:00 noon. Saturday, January 31st

WHERE? Olson's Horse Farm

WHAT?

SPORTS

Sledding   Skijoring
Snowboarding   Sleigh Rides

EATS

Real Snow Cones
Hot Cocoa and Cider
Brownies and Doughnuts
Candied Apples

ENTERTAINMENT

Western Riding Exhibition by Charlie Chase
Barrel racing by Lulu Sanders and Snow White
Snowboarding by the one, the only, Tommy Rand

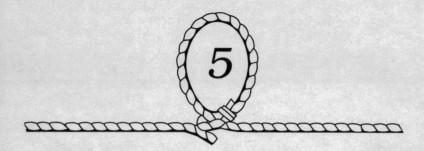

In the Night

Anna sat at the kitchen table and watched Acorn through the window. He threw back his head and whinnied as if to say, "I'm happy to be home." Then he ran around the paddock twice.

Acorn is happy because Snow White isn't here, thought Anna. Snow White might have to move to Pam's. That's okay. The Crandals have plenty of room for another pony. Lots of people have ponies that don't live right behind their houses.

Anna chewed the last bite of her tomato-

and-cheese sandwich. Lulu can ride back and forth to the Crandals' on a mountain bike, she decided. Pony Pal Trail is perfect for that.

After lunch, Anna went to her room and took out paper, paint, and brushes. I'll paint a picture of Acorn by himself in the paddock, she thought. I haven't done that in a long time.

Pam and Lulu took their ponies into the Crandals' barn to cool them down.

Mrs. Crandal came out of the office to see the girls.

"I made meatballs and sauce for dinner," she said. "Could you girls make a salad? I have another lesson to teach today."

"Sure," answered Lulu. She loved having dinner at the Crandals' and didn't mind helping out.

"Anna phoned a little while ago," Mrs. Crandal added. "She said to tell you that she can't come tonight."

"Why not?" asked Pam.

"She didn't say," answered Pam's mother. She turned and walked back into the barn.

"I'm going to call Anna," Pam told Lulu. She followed her mother into the barn and went to the office.

"Are you sick?" Pam asked Anna over the phone.

"No," answered Anna.

"So how come you're not here?" asked Pam.

"Acorn and I just want to stay home," answered Anna.

"Why?" asked Pam.

"Acorn doesn't want to be around Snow White, and I don't want to be around Lulu," admitted Anna. "But don't tell Lulu."

"Your ponies are fighting," said Pam. "That's a Pony Pal Problem. We can't solve it if you and Lulu are fighting, too."

"We're not fighting," said Anna. "We disagree. I'll see you tomorrow." She hung up.

Pam stared at the phone. There would only be two Pony Pals for dinner and the barn sleepover.

It was okay to have only two Pony Pals during dinner. But it felt strange to Pam when they went to the barn for the night.

"It feels weird to have a barn sleepover without Anna," Pam told Lulu. "We've never had one without her."

"I know," said Lulu. She slipped into her sleeping bag. Pam wishes Anna stayed over instead of me, she thought.

Pam lay awake for a long time thinking about the Pony Pal Problem. She knew why Anna and Lulu were fighting. They were defending their own ponies. But why are Snow White and Acorn fighting? she wondered.

Pam remembered how she figured out what was bothering Fat Cat. Maybe I could help Snow White and Acorn, too, she thought.

"Lulu," she said softly. There was no answer. "Lulu," she said again. Still no answer.

Pam quietly unzipped her sleeping bag and slipped out. This was her chance to be alone with Snow White.

Pam went out to the paddock where Snow White and Lightning were sleeping. Lightning was in her usual spot under the tree. Snow White was near the gate. Pam was glad that they weren't beside each other. She wanted to be totally alone with Snow White.

Pam gently brushed Snow White's face with the tips of her fingers. "Wake up, pretty pony," she whispered.

Snow White opened her eyes and nickered softly. Pam gave her a carrot. While Snow White munched, Pam tried to empty her own mind. She wouldn't think about the Wiggins Winter Fest. She wouldn't think about Anna and Lulu. She would only think about Snow White.

Next, Pam took a deep breath and relaxed.

She put her hand on Snow White's head and listened with both her heart and mind.

Pam stayed that way for a long time. Finally, an idea about Snow White came into her head. Snow White doesn't like Acorn anymore, Pam realized. She is afraid of him.

"I understand," she whispered to Snow White. "I'm going to try to solve this problem." Snow White nuzzled Pam's shoulder.

"What are you doing?" a voice asked.

Pam was startled. She turned and saw Lulu standing behind her.

"What are you doing to Snow White?" asked Lulu.

Pam felt embarrassed. "I was trying to find out why Snow White and Acorn are fighting," she said.

"They're fighting because Acorn bit her," said Lulu. "Snow White was defending herself."

"We're never going to figure out the real problem if you keep blaming Acorn instead," said Pam.

"You're taking sides because you were Anna's friend first," complained Lulu.

"What?! I am not taking sides," protested Pam. "I'm trying to find out what happened."

Lulu crossed her arms. She felt jealous of Pam. Why did Pam think she knew so much about Snow White? Snow White wasn't her pony.

"Snow White doesn't like Acorn anymore," explained Pam. "She's afraid of him. I *think* that's what she's thinking."

Lulu gave Pam a strange look. "You mean you think you know what Snow White thinks?" she asked. "Like you knew what I was thinking this afternoon?"

Pam nodded. She felt herself blush. "Sometimes I can do that," she admitted quietly. "Especially with animals."

"Did Snow White tell you who bit first?" she asked Pam.

Pam felt strange. She didn't want people to think she could talk to animals. Not even her best friends.

"I think Acorn bit Snow White first," said

Pam. "That's why Snow White's afraid of him."

"I knew that," said Lulu. She leaned her head against Snow White's neck.

"But why did Acorn bite her?" asked Pam. "Maybe Snow White upset him."

"You're taking sides again," said Lulu. "You're blaming Snow White."

Pam put her hands on her hips. "I'm not," she insisted. "I'm just trying to figure out what happened."

"If you're so good at talking to animals," said Lulu, "talk to Acorn and find out why he's being mean to Snow White. *If* he'll tell you the truth."

"I can't *talk* to animals," Pam told Lulu as they headed back to the office. "I just have this *feeling* about them."

Lulu followed her. "Like you're reading their minds?" she asked.

"That sounds too weird," said Pam. "Maybe it's like a sixth sense. Maybe I'm not even right."

"You're right about one thing," said Lulu.

"Acorn bit Snow White first. But I knew that all along."

Anna woke up three times during the night. Each time she went to the window to check on Acorn.

The first time he was sleeping in the open shed.

The second time he was sleeping near the fence.

The third time Anna checked, Acorn was back in the shed.

He didn't run away again, thought Anna. He's happy being alone. I don't mind being alone, either, she decided. It's not that much fun being a Pony Pal lately.

Tell Me Everything

When Lulu woke the next morning, Pam was already dressed. Lulu hurried and dressed, too. They went out to feed their ponies and make a plan for the day.

"Snow White and I are practicing our western riding tricks this morning," Lulu announced as they walked into the paddock.

"I should go to Anna's," said Pam. "To see Acorn."

Lulu raised an eyebrow and grinned. "Are you going to read his mind?" she asked.

Pam nodded, but she didn't smile back.

Communicating with animals was serious, and she didn't want to joke about it.

The ponies smelled the buckets of grain and ran over to the girls.

I bet Anna already knows that Pam talks to animals, thought Lulu. They've been friends since kindergarten. They probably have lots of secrets that they don't tell me.

"You go to Anna's and I'll go to Mr. Olson's," said Lulu.

"We can meet at the diner for lunch," said Pam.

The two friends headed to the house.

"I'd better call Anna and tell her I'm coming," said Pam.

"Tell her that Acorn bit Snow White first," said Lulu.

An hour later Anna sat on the paddock fence waiting for Pam. She was facing Pony Pal Trail.

When Acorn saw Lightning, he whinnied excitedly. This is going to be fun, thought Anna. It will be just me and Pam. It will be like the way it was before Lulu moved to Wiggins.

Pam rode up to Anna and dismounted.

"Could you ride Lightning up and down Pony Pal Trail?" asked Pam.

"Are you going to ride Acorn?" asked Anna, confused.

"No," answered Pam. "I just want to be alone with Acorn."

"Why?" asked Anna.

Pam didn't want to talk about communicating with animals. But if I'm going to help my friends, she thought, I have to talk about it.

"I want to communicate with Acorn," Pam said. "I'm going to ask him why he bit Snow White."

"That's easy," said Anna sarcastically. "He bit Snow White because Snow White bit him."

"Acorn bit first," said Pam.

Anna put her hands on her hips. "How do you know who did what first?" she asked. "You weren't there."

"I have this feeling," admitted Pam. "Snow White sort of told me."

Anna laughed. "Ponies don't talk, Pam," she said.

"Sometimes animals let me know what they're thinking," said Pam. "I don't know how. They just do."

Anna stared at Pam. She's serious, thought Anna.

"Maybe Acorn will tell me why he's angry at Snow White," continued Pam.

"I'll take Lightning out," agreed Anna quietly. She took Lightning's reins from Pam. "I just hope Acorn isn't jealous because I'm riding another pony."

Acorn wasn't jealous. He was happy to follow Pam and a carrot into the shed.

Meanwhile, Anna shortened the stirrups on Lightning and mounted.

As Anna rode along Pony Pal Trail, she wondered what was happening back in the paddock. Would Acorn tell Pam what was wrong? I wish Acorn would talk to me, she thought. He's my pony.

Pam faced Acorn and stroked both sides of his neck. Acorn's muscles relaxed under her hands. She took a deep breath and focused her mind on him.

Acorn, why are you angry with Snow White? Pam silently asked.

She listened with her mind and heart and closed her eyes. Images flashed in Pam's head.

Acorn watching Snow White doing tricks with Charlie and Lulu.

Charlie saying hello to Snow White and not paying attention to Acorn.

Acorn watching Snow White running with Darling.

A moonlit night. Snow White asleep in the paddock. Acorn wakes her up because he wants to play. Snow White ignores him. She's tired. Acorn nudges her. She tosses her head back in protest. Acorn bites her. Snow White bites him back.

Pam opened her eyes. So that's what happened, she thought.

Pam patted Acorn's cheek. "And when

Snow White bit you back, you ran away. You thought Lightning would be more fun?"

Pam gave Acorn another carrot and thought. Then she went to the fence to wait for Anna. She couldn't wait to tell her what she learned from Acorn.

Lulu barrel raced Snow White in a clover-leaf pattern. She noticed that two people came up to the fence line. She knew they were Tommy and Mike, but she didn't care. All she cared about was leaning into her turns.

When Lulu finished, she pulled Snow White up in front of Charlie. Charlie patted Snow White's head. "Good work," he said. He looked up at Lulu. "You, too, Lulu. You and Snow White are a good team."

Lulu grinned. "Thanks," she said.

Tommy and Mike and two snowboards were leaning against the fence.

"Hey, can we put the pony away now and hit the snow?" asked Tommy.

Charlie looked from Tommy to Lulu.

"Go ahead," she said. "Snow White could use a rest."

"You should come, too," Charlie told Lulu.

"You'd be a good snowboarder, Pony Pest," said Tommy. "You got good balance."

Lulu couldn't believe her ears. Tommy Rand actually gave her a compliment — sort of.

"Thanks, but I'll stay with Snow White," said Lulu.

Lulu put Snow White in the paddock with Darling. The leggy filly ran over to greet her. Snow White led the way in a happy gallop around the paddock.

Tommy, Mike, and Charlie were hooting and hollering on the snowy hill.

Lulu missed her Pony Pals.

Anna and Pam sat in the Harley kitchen drinking hot chocolate. Pam told Anna everything she learned from Acorn.

"Acorn is used to being the center of attention," said Anna.

"That's right," agreed Pam. She dropped

another marshmallow in her hot chocolate. "So we know what the problem is."

"What should we do about it?" asked Anna.

"We need three good ideas," answered Pam. "We can share them at lunch."

"What about Lulu?" asked Anna.

"I'll call her at Mr. Olson's," explained Pam.

Anna looked at her watch. "My tutor's coming here at eleven. But you don't have to go home."

While Anna worked with her tutor in the kitchen, Pam went up to Anna's room. First, she called Lulu at Mr. Olson's. She told her what she learned from Acorn and about their Pony Pal lunch meeting. Next, she worked on her own idea and wrote it down.

Pam stared out the window and thought about communicating with the two ponies. That made her think about other times that she had sensed what animals were thinking or feeling. She tried to remember the first time she did it.

I want to write this down, she thought, so I'll never forget.

Pam turned to a new page in her Pony Pal notebook, picked up her pen, and began to write.

I have learned something important about myself. I can communicate with animals, especially ponies.

I remember something that happened a few years ago. My mom's horse, JB, started to eat wood. No one knew why.

I went into JB's stall when no one else was in the barn. I touched his neck, looked into his eyes, and asked him why he was eating the window ledge. I waited and listened. Suddenly, I knew the answer. I didn't hear words. Animals don't use words.

The goat pen had been near JB's stall window. But we had moved it to the other side of the barn. I suddenly understood that JB was lonely and sad because he missed Queenie, one of our goats.

I told my mother. She moved JB to a stall where he could see the new goat pen. JB stopped eating the barn.

My mother knows all about horses and ponies and is very good with them. I was surprised that JB didn't tell my mom what was wrong.

Now I think I know why Acorn and Snow White are fighting. Here are my ideas:

Acorn is used to being the center of attention. He's the pony who knows tricks. Snow White is learning tricks in western riding.

Acorn doesn't understand why Snow White is suddenly getting so much attention.

Snow White is also tired from working in western riding and playing with Darling. She is too tired to play with Acorn.

Acorn is confused and angry with Snow White. Why is Snow White learning tricks? he wonders. Why does Snow White have a new friend? Why won't Snow White play with me?

Snow White is confused, too. She doesn't understand why Acorn is acting mean to her. So she's angry at Acorn, and a little afraid.

I was surprised that I understood what was bothering Snow White and Acorn.

I didn't want to tell anyone that I can communicate with animals. They might think I'm weird — or that I'm making it up. I wish nobody knew. But now Anna and Lulu do.

Anna and Lulu are fighting. I think that Anna is jealous of Lulu because she is doing tricks. I wonder if Lulu is jealous about something, too? It is easier for me to understand animals than people.

I hope I never lose this special gift, even if I only use it some of the time. I know I can't understand everything about animals. Not all animals will talk to me. Sometimes I can't hear them. Not even Lightning. But I will always try.

Three Ideas

Lulu rode up to the diner and saw Lightning alone at the hitching post. She tied Snow White next to her then looked behind the diner. Acorn was at the fence. Lulu was glad that Snow White would have a turn at the hitching post. I bet it was Pam's idea, she thought.

Pam and Anna were waiting for Lulu in the diner.

"Hi," said Pam. "How was practice?"

"Great," answered Lulu. She didn't look at Anna.

Lulu and Anna didn't even say hi to each other, thought Pam. She hated that her two best friends were fighting.

"We're having hamburger platters," Pam told Lulu. "What do you want?"

"The same," answered Lulu. "And milk."

While Anna placed the order, Pam and Lulu put silverware and napkins on the table and sat facing each other.

"Did you tell Anna that Acorn started the fight?" asked Lulu.

"Nobody started it," said Pam. "It just started. Like your fight with Anna."

As Anna walked back to the booth, she heard Lulu say, "I'm sick of Anna blaming Snow White."

Anna sat next to Pam and glared at Lulu. "And I'm sick of you blaming Acorn," she said angrily.

"Acorn started it," said Lulu.

Pam held up her hands to stop the arguing. "Okay, okay," she said. "Let's *start* our meeting and try to solve this problem. Lulu, what's your idea?"

Lulu took a folded piece of paper from her jeans pocket. She read her idea out loud.

Acorn is used to being the star. Now he's jealous of Snow White. We have to give Acorn more attention.

"Acorn is not a show-off!" exclaimed Anna.

"He doesn't want anyone else to learn tricks," said Lulu.

"That's not being a show-off," said Anna.

"I never said he was a show-off," protested Lulu. "You said it. I said he was *jealous*."

"Well, he's not jealous, either," said Anna angrily.

"Three Pony Pal Burger Specials on board," the cook shouted.

"I'll get them," said Anna and Lulu in unison. They both stood up.

"At least you agree on something," said Pam. She stood up, too. "I'll get our drinks."

Anna and Lulu went to the kitchen.

I'm never going to speak to Anna again, thought Lulu. Everything I say makes her angry.

I'm never going to speak to Lulu again, thought Anna. Everything I say makes her angry.

They ate without speaking.

Pam finally broke the silence. "Lulu's idea is good," she said.

Anna scowled at Pam.

"But you're wrong about one thing, Lulu," continued Pam. "Acorn isn't *jealous*. He's *confused* because Snow White is learning tricks. We have to remind Acorn that he's special, too."

"That's what I meant," said Lulu.

"What's your idea, Anna?" asked Pam.

Anna took out her drawing and handed it to Pam. Pam put it on the table so Lulu could see, too.

"Snow White and Acorn shouldn't share a

paddock right now," explained Anna. "Snow White can live with Lightning."

Lulu hated Anna's idea. "Why does Snow White have to move?" she asked. "Acorn's the one who ran away. He's the one who wants to be with Lightning."

"Because it was Acorn's paddock first!" exclaimed Anna. "And it's *my* backyard. That's why!"

"I don't think it's a good idea," said Pam.

Anna glared at her.

"Listen to me," continued Pam. "Acorn shouldn't be alone. He needs a stablemate.

When he didn't have one, he was always jumping out and running away. It was a big problem."

Lulu remembered how she first met Acorn. It was the middle of the night and Acorn had jumped into her grandmother's garden. The mischievous pony ate her grandmother's favorite flowers and her grandmother was really angry. Lulu started to giggle.

"What's so funny?" asked Anna, annoyed.

"Remember when Acorn ate my grandmother's geraniums?" asked Lulu. "We were all in our pajamas — even my grandmother. And her hair was sticking out all over. She was so angry and she looked so silly. I was trying not to laugh."

Anna smiled. "Me, too," she remembered. "But she scared me."

Pam took out her notebook and started writing.

Anna tapped her on the arm. "I thought you already had an idea," she said.

"I did," said Pam. "I'm just adding something."

When Pam finished writing, she handed her idea to Lulu. Lulu read it out loud.

Anna and Lulu have to work on this problem together. If they're not friends, their ponies won't be friends.

Anna and Lulu should write down all the great things their ponies have done together.

"I think Acorn and Snow White are still fighting because you are still fighting," Pam told Anna and Lulu. "Animals pick up on how people feel."

"But we're fighting because our ponies are," said Lulu.

"It's a vicious circle," agreed Pam.

Anna made a circle out of a drinking straw. "How do we stop it?" she asked.

"It might help if you and Lulu remember the good times you and your ponies had to-

gether," explained Pam. "You could even write them down. Maybe you could make a pony journal."

Lulu ate a french fry and thought. "Maybe," she said.

"Acorn and Snow White used to be great friends," added Anna as she twirled the straw circle on her finger.

"Lulu, you've taken some great pictures of Snow White and Acorn," said Pam. "You could put those in the journal."

"That would make a pony journal special," added Anna. "It would be more like a scrapbook."

"Will you do some drawings?" Lulu asked Anna. "You're the best artist."

"Sure," agreed Anna. "But Lightning should be in the pony journal, too."

"I was just thinking the same thing," said Lulu.

Pam smiled to herself. It already feels like we're Pony Pals again, she thought. "We can write our ponies' adventures from the ponies' point of view," she said.

"They'll tell their own stories," agreed Lulu.

"Like *Black Beauty*," added Anna. "That's my favorite horse book."

"Mine, too," said Lulu.

Lulu picked up the straw circle and twirled it on her finger.

"I hope Acorn and Snow White stop fighting," she said.

"Me, too," agreed Anna.

Anna and Lulu smiled at each other. It was great to be friends again.

Pam leaned forward. "Don't look now," she said. "But trouble just walked in the door."

Lulu and Anna looked anyway. Tommy, Mike, and Charlie were coming toward them.

"There's only two ponies outside," said Tommy. "Did one of the little Pony Pests lose her little pony?"

"Where's Acorn?" asked Charlie.

"He's out back," answered Pam.

Lulu and Anna exchanged a glance. They were thinking the same thing. Acorn and Snow White couldn't even be at the same hitching post. Would they ever be friends again?

Cold and Fluffy

Tommy grinned at Anna. "There're so many Pony Pests here," he said. "Your mother should hire an exterminator."

The girls and Charlie ignored Tommy. Even Mike didn't laugh at Tommy's dumb joke.

Charlie sat down next to Lulu. Mike started to squeeze in beside Anna.

Tommy grabbed Mike's arm and yanked him back up. "Come on," he growled. "We've got better things to do."

The Pony Pals exchanged a glance.

They all hated that Tommy ordered Mike around.

"You coming?" Tommy asked Charlie.

"Nope," answered Charlie.

But Mike still followed Tommy toward the door.

"See you at the Winter Fest tomorrow," Charlie called after them.

"Yeah, yeah," Tommy said over his shoulder. "Whatever."

"What's wrong with those guys?" Charlie asked the Pony Pals. "Sometimes they're okay and sometimes they're sort of dumb."

"They are *very* dumb around us," said Pam.

"*All the time*," added Anna.

Lulu pushed her plate toward Charlie. "Want some fries?" she asked.

Charlie shared the rest of Lulu's fries while he waited for a burger. He pointed to the papers on the table. "What are those?" he asked. "More ideas for the Winter Fest?"

"They're ideas for helping Acorn and Snow White be friends again," answered Lulu.

"Did you figure out why they're fighting?" asked Charlie.

"Pam did," answered Anna.

Pam elbowed Anna to keep quiet. But it was too late.

"She talked to them," explained Lulu.

Anna told Charlie what Pam learned from Snow White and Acorn.

"That's what I thought," agreed Charlie. "And I have the perfect solution to this problem."

Here he goes again, thought Pam. Charlie Chase — the boy who knows everything.

Anna rolled her eyes at Pam. Lulu raised her right eyebrow. They agreed that Charlie was acting like a know-it-all.

"So what's your idea, Charlie?" asked Lulu.

"It's brilliant," said Charlie enthusiastically. "Acorn can demonstrate some of his tricks at the Winter Fest." He smiled at Anna. "Then you'll be in the show, too."

"What about Pam and Lightning?" asked Anna.

"They can demonstrate jumping," suggested Lulu.

"Pam and Lightning are a great jumping team," Anna told Charlie.

Pam smiled. "Okay," she agreed. "We can do jumps."

"Acorn should practice his tricks this afternoon," said Lulu. "That's part of the plan." She turned to Charlie. "Right?"

"Right," he agreed. "Then he'll know that he's still a star."

Lulu and Pam rode to Olson's Horse Farm together.

Anna followed on Acorn. Charlie jogged beside her. Anna wondered if her pony missed riding with his friends.

When they all reached Mr. Olson's, Anna brought Acorn into the ring.

Acorn turned and looked at Snow White. Snow White backed up and her ears flattened. She's still afraid of him, thought Lulu.

Anna demonstrated all of Acorn's tricks

for Charlie. When they'd finished, Acorn bowed in front of him.

Charlie, Pam, and Lulu clapped enthusiastically.

Acorn *is* a very talented pony, thought Lulu.

Next, Pam and Lightning practiced jumping. Lulu helped set up a course of jumps.

"This is great," said Charlie. "Three new acts for the show." He smiled at Lulu.

"Three?" said Lulu.

"You're going to demonstrate barrel racing," he explained.

"I am?" asked Lulu.

"Of course you are!" answered Pam and Anna enthusiastically.

Acorn whinnied as if to agree.

"Let's bring Snow White over to Acorn," suggested Pam. "This is a good time."

"Okay," agreed Lulu. She gave Snow White a reassuring pat.

Anna slowly led Acorn toward Lulu's pony. "Hi, Snow White," she called cheerfully.

Snow White backed up a few paces.

"Everything is all right," said Lulu soothingly. She patted Snow White's neck again. "Anna and Acorn are our friends."

Lulu reached out and stroked Acorn's muzzle. He raised his eyes and gazed at her. "You're such a good pony," she said.

Acorn reached his nose toward Snow White and sniffed.

"Two wonderful ponies," said Lulu soothingly.

"It's your friend, Acorn," Lulu reminded Snow White.

Snow White didn't back up. She sniffed Acorn back.

Acorn nickered as if to say, "Friends?"

Snow White's ears flickered happily.

Anna and Lulu exchanged a big smile. Their ponies were friends again.

"It's snowing!" Pam exclaimed.

Lulu saw big fluffy snowflakes falling on her jacket sleeve.

Anna stuck out her tongue and felt cold flakes land and melt.

"It's coming down pretty fast," observed Charlie.

Pam pulled up the hood on her jacket. "We'd better go home," she said.

Just then Mr. Olson came out of the barn. He looked up at the quickly falling snow. "Storm came up pretty sudden," he said. "Could be a big one."

"Can we still have the Winter Fest if it's snowing?" asked Lulu.

Mr. Olson shook his head. "Roads won't be clear," he explained. "Parking would be messed up."

"Let's saddle up," Pam told Anna and Lulu. "Pretty soon it won't be safe to ride."

Mr. Olson looked up at the sky again. "It isn't safe now," he said. "This could turn into a blizzard before you get home. You better leave your ponies here tonight. I'll give you girls a ride home in the pickup."

"Can the Pony Pals stay, too?" Charlie asked his uncle.

"Sure," answered Mr. Olson. "But if the

snow doesn't stop, we can't have the Winter Fest."

"Will you stay?" asked Charlie.

The Pony Pals glanced at one another.

Pam and Anna nodded.

Lulu made an okay sign.

"We'll stay," announced Pam. "Can we sleep in your office? We love barn sleep-overs."

"Fine with me," said Mr. Olson. "I've slept out there plenty myself. Especially during foaling time."

"But what about our stuff?" asked Anna.

"Our sleeping bags are at Pam's," explained Lulu.

"And we need our outfits for the Winter Fest," added Anna. "If there is one."

"We'll go for them now," said Mr. Olson. "Before this storm gets too bad. We'll buy groceries, too." He put an arm around Charlie. "Mr. Charlie can make you his special Mexican burritos."

"They're *muy delicioso*," bragged Charlie.

"I'll put our ponies in the barn," offered Lulu.

"I'll help you," said Charlie.

Pam smiled at Mr. Olson. "Anna and I will get our stuff," she said, "and help you shop."

As Anna climbed into Mr. Olson's pickup truck, an idea flashed into her mind. "Let's get our pony photos and my art supplies, too," she told Pam. "We can work on our pony journal tonight."

"Perfect," agreed Pam. "I have a scrapbook we can use."

An hour later, Charlie and the Pony Pals were in the kitchen. While Charlie made the burritos, the Pony Pals worked on their pony journal. Pam had her notebook and the new scrapbook opened in front of her. Anna was drawing. Lulu was going through a box of photographs.

The girls told Charlie stories about their ponies. Pam wrote the stories on scrap paper. Then she and Lulu helped edit them.

Next, Lulu read the stories aloud. Finally, Pam wrote them down in the scrapbook.

Mr. Olson came in to get a drink. The stories were so interesting he stayed to listen.

By the time dinner was ready, the Pony Friends Scrapbook was finished. Five inches of snow had already fallen.

Anna looked out the window at the swirling snow. If it doesn't stop, there won't be a Winter Fest tomorrow, she thought.

ACORN, SNOW WHITE, AND LIGHTNING
ARE FRIENDS 4-EVER

I USED TO LIVE ALONE IN MY PADDOCK. MY OWNER, ANNA, IS GREAT. BUT SHE GOES TO SCHOOL AND SLEEPS IN THE HOUSE. SO I WAS LONELY AND BORED — ESPECIALLY AT NIGHT. SOMETIMES I'D JUMP OUT OF THE PADDOCK. I'D GO TO THE NEIGHBOR'S YARDS AND EAT THEIR FLOWERS. THEY WERE YUMMY. THEN SNOW WHITE MOVED IN WITH ME. NOW I'M NEVER LONELY OR BORED.

ACORN

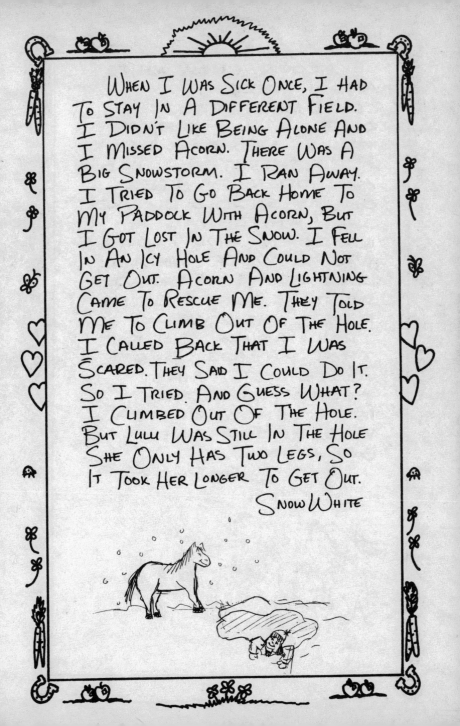

WHEN I WAS SICK ONCE, I HAD
TO STAY IN A DIFFERENT FIELD.
I DIDN'T LIKE BEING ALONE AND
I MISSED ACORN. THERE WAS A
BIG SNOWSTORM. I RAN AWAY.
I TRIED TO GO BACK HOME TO
MY PADDOCK WITH ACORN, BUT
I GOT LOST IN THE SNOW. I FELL
IN AN ICY HOLE AND COULD NOT
GET OUT. ACORN AND LIGHTNING
CAME TO RESCUE ME. THEY TOLD
ME TO CLIMB OUT OF THE HOLE.
I CALLED BACK THAT I WAS
SCARED. THEY SAID I COULD DO IT.
SO I TRIED. AND GUESS WHAT?
I CLIMBED OUT OF THE HOLE.
BUT LULU WAS STILL IN THE HOLE
SHE ONLY HAS TWO LEGS, SO
IT TOOK HER LONGER TO GET OUT.

SNOW WHITE

ACORN, SNOW WHITE, AND I WERE IN A COSTUME PARADE ONCE. I WAS A FIRE TRUCK AND PAM WAS A FIREFIGHTER. I HAD A LADDER PAINTED ON MY SADDLE BLANKET. SNOW WHITE WAS A UNICORN, AND ACORN WAS A WOLF. WE ALL LOVE BEING IN PARADES. WE TAKE TURNS BEING FIRST WHEN WE GO TRAIL RIDING. BUT FOR THAT PARADE, SNOW WHITE WENT FIRST. ACORN AND I DIDN'T MIND. SNOW WHITE WAS PROUD AND BEAUTIFUL.

LIGHTNING

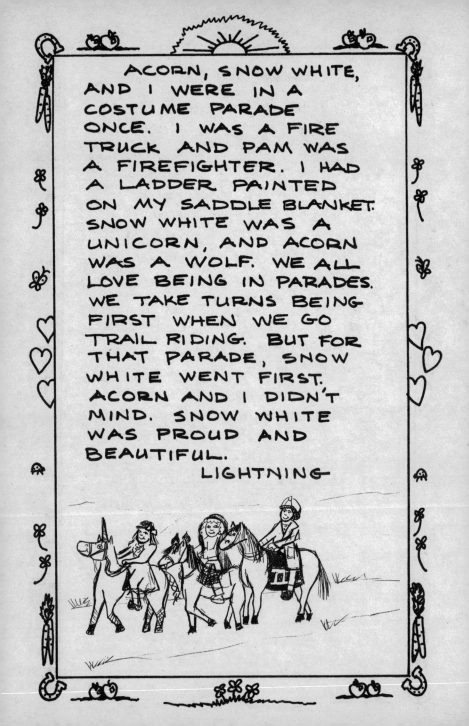

TOMMY RAND AND
MIKE LACEY STOLE US
ONCE. TOMMY USED
TO OWN ME. HE WAS
NICER WHEN HE WAS
YOUNGER. ANYWAY, WE
DIDN'T LIKE BEING WITH
THOSE BOYS. THEY DIDN'T
FEED US TREATS OR
TALK NICE TO US OR DO
ANY OF THE GOOD STUFF
THE PONY PALS DO. WE
WERE AFRAID THAT THE
PONY PALS WOULDN'T
FIND US IN THE WOODS.
I KEPT TELLING SNOW
WHITE AND LIGHTNING
THAT WE'D BE OKAY.
BUT I DIDN'T BELIEVE
IT MYSELF. THOSE BOYS
ARE ALWAYS DOING
STUPID AND DANGEROUS
THINGS, EVEN WHEN THEY
DON'T THINK THEY ARE.
SUDDENLY, I HEARD A
SIGNAL FROM ANNA.
SHE WAS CALLING ME
FROM ACROSS THE

BROOK. I COULDN'T SEE
HER, BUT I KNEW SHE
WAS THERE. THE
BROOK WAS RUNNING
FAST, BUT I DIDN'T
CARE. I RAN ACROSS IT.
WHILE THE BOYS WERE
YELLING AT ANNA AND
ME, PAM AND LULU
RESCUED SNOW WHITE
AND LIGHTNING. IT WAS
AN EXCITING DAY. I
LOVE EXCITEMENT.
SNOW WHITE WISHES
IT HAD NEVER HAPPENED.
WE ARE DIFFERENT
THAT WAY.

ACORN

One morning, the three of us were going on a trip with the Pony Pals. Lightning was already in the trailer when Acorn and I got there. I hate trailers and did not want to go inside. Lightning told us it was okay and to come on in. I didn't go in until Acorn did. Then I walked in very slowly. It was okay in there because I was with my two best friends.

Snow White

I HAVE A LOT OF ANIMAL FRIENDS. I HAVE A DOG THE PEOPLE CALL "WOOLIE." I CALL HIM "NUISANCE." HE'S ALWAYS GETTING UNDER HOOF. I HAVE A CAT, TOO. AND A BUNCH OF KITTENS. THE CAT'S NAME IS FAT CAT. FAT CAT HAD HER KITTENS IN MY SHED. I PROTECTED THEM. ONCE, I FOUND A BABY LAMB ON OUR PONY TRAIL. THE LITTLE THING WAS LOST AND WOULD HAVE DIED. BUT I TOLD PAM ABOUT IT AND WE SAVED ITS LIFE.

PAM LOVES ALL KINDS
OF ANIMALS, TOO. BUT
SNOW WHITE AND ACORN
ARE OUR FAVORITES.
THEY'RE MY BEST
FRIENDS. WE HAVE
WONDERFUL ADVENTURES
WITH THE PONY PALS.
                    LIGHTNING

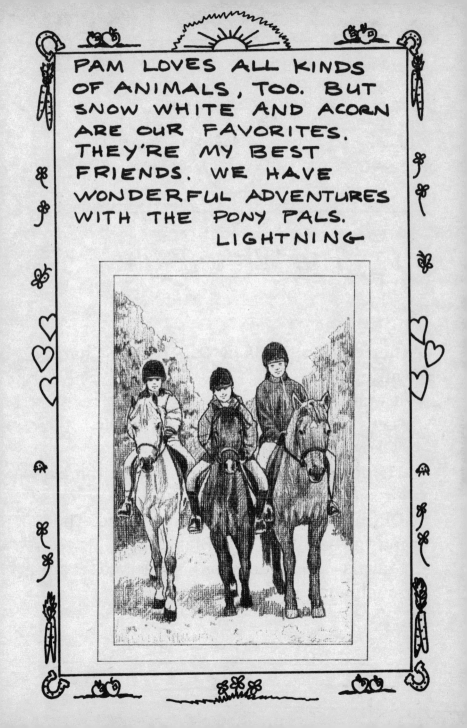

The White Fight

After dinner, the Pony Pals helped Charlie clean up.

It was still snowing.

"Let's play cards," suggested Charlie.

"Okay," agreed the Pony Pals.

The four friends sat in a circle on the living room floor and played Hearts.

During the fifth game, Lulu yawned. Then Anna yawned. Next, Charlie yawned.

"Yawns are catching," observed Pam through a yawn of her own.

"We should turn in," said Charlie. "There's a lot to do tomorrow."

"If it stops snowing," said Anna and Lulu in unison.

The Pony Pals said good night to Charlie and went out to the barn.

The snow was coming down harder than ever.

Mr. Olson's barn office was cozy and warm. The three friends laid their sleeping bags out side by side.

Then they went to the stalls to say good night to their ponies.

Snow White's and Acorn's heads were sticking out of the stall. They sniffed and nuzzled each other.

"They are best friends again," said Pam.

Lightning's head was out of the stall, too. But no one was sniffing or nuzzling her.

"I hope Lightning isn't jealous," said Lulu.

Anna turned to Pam. "Ask Lightning if she's jealous," she said.

"Okay," agreed Pam. "I'll try."

Anna and Lulu stood back while Pam communicated with her pony.

She took a deep breath and concentrated. The thought of Lightning filled her heart and mind.

After a short while, Pam turned to her friends. "Lightning isn't jealous," she said. "She's happy that everyone is friends again." She smiled at Anna and Lulu. "Me, too."

"Pam, how do you know what Lightning's thinking?" asked Anna.

"Tell us how you do it," added Lulu.

"Okay," agreed Pam.

When the Pony Pals were ready for bed, they sat cross-legged on their sleeping bags. Pam hoped that she could explain how she communicated with animals. She told her friends about emptying her head of other thoughts. She described taking a deep breath and trying to relax.

"Wait a minute," said Lulu. She reached for her backpack and took out her notebook. "I want to write this down."

"Me, too," said Anna. She took out her sketchbook.

Anna and Lulu wrote down Pam's steps to communication with animals.

STEPS TO BETTER
ANIMAL COMMUNICATION
1) Clear your head
2) Breathe deeply and slowly
3) Focus on the animal
4) Relax and listen
5) Believe what you learn

"Animal communication must take a lot of practice," concluded Lulu.

"I bet some people can do it better than others," added Anna.

"Probably," agreed Pam. "And sometimes I can't do it at all. Especially if I'm worried about Lightning."

She stretched her arms and yawned.

Anna and Lulu got into their sleeping

bags. Pam turned out the light before slip-
ping into hers.

The three friends lay in the dark.

"Please don't tell anyone that I talk to animals," said Pam. "Okay?"

"Okay," agreed Anna and Lulu in unison.

"Good night," whispered Anna.

"Good night," said Pam.

"See you in the morning," said Lulu.

Pam was the first to wake the next morning.

It was still snowing.

"Too bad," said Pam with a sigh.

Anna turned over in her sleeping bag and
looked up at Pam. "It's still snowing?" she
asked.

"Yeah," said Pam as she turned from the
window.

Lulu sat up and looked out the window,
too. "It's still coming down hard," she said.

The girls used the bathroom, dressed, and
rolled up their sleeping bags.

When they finished, it was still snowing.

"Guess we'll have to cancel the Winter Fest," said Anna.

Lulu looked at her watch. "It's only seven-thirty," she said. "Maybe the snow will stop in time."

BANG! Something hit the window.

Anna jumped back.

"What was that?" asked Lulu, looking around.

BANG! SPLAT! The window rattled.

"Snowballs!" exclaimed Pam.

The girls exchanged a glance. It was an Instant Pony Pal Meeting. They all knew what they had to do. Anna-the-actress went out the front door of the barn. Meanwhile, Lulu and Pam snuck out the back.

"Hey," Anna called. "Hey, who's out there?" she called as she scooped up snow from the windowsill and quickly packed a snowball. "Who hit the window?"

SPLAT! A snowball caught Anna on her arm. Spinning around she hurled her snow-ball at Charlie Chase.

In the same instant, Lulu and Pam hit him from behind.

"Truce! Truce!" shouted Charlie.

"No way," shouted Anna as she threw another snowball.

Charlie ducked. The snowball hit Pam on the leg.

Pam threw her snow weapon at Anna.

Snowballs flew through the air. There were no sides. Just hitting and being hit.

Mr. Olson opened the kitchen door. "Cease fire!" he shouted.

The snowball fight continued.

"PANCAKES!" Mr. Olson shouted.

The snowballs suddenly stopped flying. Four snow-warriors ran into the house.

"We already have an accumulation of seven inches," Mr. Olson announced as he served up pancakes and scrambled eggs.

"That would be great for the Winter Fest," said Charlie.

"If it would just stop falling," said his uncle.

"If it stops this morning, can we still have

the Winter Fest this afternoon?" asked Anna.

"It would have to stop in the next hour," said Mr. Olson.

Lulu looked out the window at the falling snow. It looked like it would never stop.

Snow Pony

The phone rang. Mr. Olson answered it.

"I'm giving it until ten o'clock," he told the caller. "Listen to WKTZ radio. They'll make an announcement if the festival is cancelled."

Mr. Olson leaned against the refrigerator. "That was the man who's lending us the bleachers," he said.

Pam slumped back in her chair and thought about all the work they'd done for the Winter Fest.

Anna rested her face in her hand. Her

mother had made dozens of brownies. What would happen to them?

Lulu pushed the last piece of pancake around her plate. She thought about all the kids who would be disappointed.

"Wow!" said Charlie. "Everyone looks *so* depressed."

The Pony Pals looked at one another. They needed something to cheer everyone up.

An idea popped into Anna's head. "Let's make a snow pony," she said.

"The snow is perfect for that," commented Charlie. "It's not too soft."

"We can make it next to the Olson's Horse Farm sign," said Lulu.

"Good idea," agreed Mr. Olson.

The four friends put on jackets and mittens and went outside.

"Let's put a real harness on the snow pony!" shouted Pam as they ran through the swirling snow.

They rolled huge balls of snow and piled them on top of one another. Charlie, Lulu, and Pam shaped the legs and body. Anna sculpted the neck and head.

The four snow artists stood back to admire their work.

"It's a really cute pony," commented Pam.

"Now for the finishing touches," said Anna.

Pam found stones for the pony's eyes and nostrils.

Lulu curved a twig for its mouth.

Anna and Charlie went to the barn for some dried corn stalks. They pulled out the corn silk. It was perfect for the mane and tail.

Anna put on the harness.

"It looks like Snow White," observed Lulu. "You did a great job, Anna."

"Thanks," said Anna softly.

Pam looked up at the sky. It was turning bright blue. "It stopped snowing," she announced.

Lulu checked her watch. "It isn't ten o'clock yet," she said with a smile.

Anna heard the *scrape-clang* of a snowplow in the distance. "The plows are coming through!" she shouted.

The four friends cheered and hit high fives. There would be a Winter Fest after all!

"We better get back to the barn," said Charlie. "There's a lot of work to do."

As they were running up the driveway, a snowball hit Lulu on the back. "Hey!" she shouted in surprise.

Lulu could see Pam, Anna, and Charlie ahead of her. None of them had thrown it.

As she swung around, another snowball hit her on the leg.

Tommy and Mike were racing up the driveway toward her.

Lulu quickly packed a snowball and threw it. It caught Tommy in the belly.

A snowball flew past Lulu's head and hit its target — Mike's backside as he bent over.

"Good shot, Pam," shouted Charlie.

Snowballs flew through the air for several minutes.

Suddenly, Charlie put both arms up in the air. "CEASE FIRE!" he shouted. "We have work to do."

Everyone stopped. Except Tommy.

He hurled another snowball at Charlie. It caught him on the cheek. Tommy was already making another snowball.

"Drop that," said Charlie in a fierce, adult voice. "We have work to do, and we need your help."

The Pony Pals glared at Tommy. Mike looked at the ground.

Tommy dropped the snowball. "So, what's the big deal?" he asked. "What are you all standing around for? You heard him. There's work to do. Let's get started."

Tommy and Charlie made ski trails for skijoring with a snowmobile.

The town plow cleared Mr. Olson's driveway and parking spaces.

Anna and Pam groomed the ponies for the demonstrations.

Mike and Lulu organized the barn office for the refreshments.

By noon, the Pony Pals were in the house cleaning up and changing clothes.

Lulu put on fresh jeans, a plaid shirt, and a suede jacket. Pam wore her best riding pants and boots, a white blouse, and a black riding jacket. Anna wore riding pants and a big, red sweater.

Lulu glanced out the window. "A bunch of people are coming here on cross-country skis!" she shouted. "And there's Ms. Wiggins. She's driving Beauty in a sleigh."

Anna came up beside Lulu. "There are already a bunch of cars," she said. Then she pointed. "And look, people pulling their kids on sleds."

Pam joined her friends at the window. "There's the truck with the bleachers," she said. Her stomach turned a flip. She always had stomach butterflies before a riding exhibition or competition.

There was a knock on the door. "Okay," shouted Charlie. "Let's go. It's show time."

At twelve-thirty the equestrian demonstration began.

The big side doors on the indoor ring were opened. An audience waited on the bleachers facing the ring.

Mr. Olson ran out to the center of the ring. He welcomed everyone to the Wiggins Winter Fest. The audience cheered. "We open the riding demonstrations," he announced, "with Pam Crandal and her pony, Lightning."

First, Pam and Lightning did four jumps.

"That girl is a fabulous equestrian," Lulu heard Mr. Olson tell Pam's mother. And she's a fabulous friend, thought Lulu. To people and to animals.

As Pam left the ring, she smiled and waved to her parents and sister and brother. A reporter from the *Wiggins Gazette* took her picture. This is so much fun, thought Pam.

Mr. Olson announced Acorn and Anna. Anna went out to the ring. Acorn followed without a lead. Anna stopped. Acorn stopped. She went forward a few steps. Acorn took a few steps. Anna stopped. Acorn stopped.

Next, Anna gave Acorn the signal to gallop around the ring. He did it. Whenever she told him to stop, he did. She called him to her. He came. The crowd loved it.

"Acorn's the best," a kid in a striped cap shouted. Acorn bowed. Everyone applauded again.

As Anna and Acorn left the ring, Tommy, Mike, and Pam rolled three metal barrels in place.

Mr. Olson went back to center ring. "Ladies and gentlemen, boys and girls," he said, "next we have barrel racing by Lulu Sanders. Her mount has a perfect name for our Winter Fest. Please welcome Snow White and Lulu!"

"Let's go," Lulu said to Snow White as she pressed her heels. They raced right and left around the barrels. Charlie looked at his stopwatch and gave Lulu a thumbs-up. "Twenty-two seconds," he shouted to the crowd. They cheered.

Lulu and Snow White ran the course again. "Twenty seconds!" Charlie shouted when they'd finished. "They beat their own time!"

Mr. Olson rode out to the center of the ring on his horse, Handsome. "My nephew, Charlie Chase," Mr. Olson told the crowd, "will demonstrate vaulting and the Hippodrome Stand on Lulu Sanders's pony, Snow White. Handsome is the lead horse. We'll ride ahead of Snow White to keep her steady."

Mr. Olson galloped Handsome around the ring. Charlie rode out on Snow White and followed his uncle. Charlie was riding without reins and smiling. Suddenly, he threw his right leg over the saddle horn and jumped to the ground. His feet landed in front of Snow White's left shoulder. In an instant he was back in the saddle. Snow White kept moving at an even gallop throughout the trick.

The crowd cheered.

Next, Charlie did a double vault. First, he jumped off Snow White to the right, then to the left. The crowd went wild.

Lulu held her breath as Charlie squatted on top of Snow White and slipped his feet into a strap behind the saddle horn. Charlie stood on Snow White's back. He put his hands up in front of him as he rode around the ring.

The crowd didn't applaud until Charlie was safely seated in the saddle again. Then they went crazy.

As Charlie rode out of the ring, Mr. Olson rode back to the center. He waited for the applause to die down. "I direct your attention," he announced, "to the hill on your right."

Everyone in the bleachers looked to their right.

"Mommy, look!" a small child shouted.

The Pony Pals led their ponies out of the barn so they could watch, too.

Tommy Rand was snowboarding down the hill. The snowboard barely touched the ground as he swayed in and out of two rows of red flags. To Lulu it looked like he was flying.

Tommy stopped at the bottom of the hill and lifted his snowboard over his head. The *Wiggins Gazette* reporter took his picture.

The Pony Pals looked at one another in amazement.

"At least he can do something right," said Anna.

The crowd went wild. They clapped and chanted, "Tom-my. Tom-my." Meanwhile, Tommy climbed the hill to snowboard down again.

After Tommy's demonstration, Mr. Olson made his final announcement. "The rest of the afternoon is yours, my friends," he said. "Skijoring, sledding, skiing, refreshments, and sleigh rides. Enjoy."

The Pony Pals led their ponies to the front of the barn. Charlie helped Anna hitch Acorn to a sleigh. Pam and Lulu put harnesses on their ponies for skijoring.

People were trudging up the hill with sleds. Ms. Wiggins was giving the Crandal twins a sleigh ride. There were people drinking hot chocolate and cider. Anna's mother and Mike were selling brownies and doughnuts.

The reporter from the *Wiggins Gazette* came over to the Pony Pals. "Mr. Olson tells me you girls helped organize this event," she said. "Congratulations." She held up her camera. "I'd like to take your picture."

"Can we take it with our ponies?" asked Lulu.

"Sure," agreed the reporter. "If I can fit you all in."

Pam and Lulu pulled their ponies close to Acorn. The three girls leaned toward the ponies.

"That's great," said the reporter. "It's perfect that you're riding friends. That'll be a good angle for the story."

"Our ponies are friends, too," said Anna.

"Best friends," added Lulu.

Acorn sniffed Snow White. Snow White moved her face closer to Acorn's. Lightning nickered happily.

Pam put an arm around each of her friends.

The reporter snapped the picture.

Dear Reader,

I am having fun researching and writing the Pony Pal books. I've met great kids and wonderful ponies at homes, farms, and riding schools. Some of my ideas for Pony Pal adventures have even come from these visits.

I remember the day I made up the main characters for the series. I was walking on a country road in New England. First, I decided that the three girls would be smart, independent, and kind. Then I gave them their names—Pam, Anna, and Lulu. (Look at the initial of each girl's name. See what it spells when you put them together.) Later, I created the three ponies. When I reached home, I turned on my computer and started to write. And I haven't stopped since!

My friends say that I am a little bit like all of the Pony Pals. I am very organized, like Pam. I love nature, like Lulu. But I think that I am most like Anna. I am dyslexic and a good artist, just like her.

Readers often wonder about my life. I live in an apartment in New York City near Central Park and the Museum of Natural History. I enjoy swimming, hiking, painting, and reading. I also love to make up stories. I have been writing novels for children and young adults for more than twenty years! Several of my books have won the Children's Choice Award.

Many Pony Pal readers send me letters, drawings, and photos. I tape them to the wall in my office. They inspire me to write more Pony Pal stories. Thank you very much!

I don't ride anymore and I've never had a pony. But you don't have to ride to love ponies! And you certainly don't need a pony to be a Pony Pal.

Happy Reading,

Jeanne Betancourt

Note from the Author

In this SUPER SPECIAL, the ponies tell their own stories in a pony journal. You'll find the Pony Pal versions of these stories in Pony Pal books #1: I WANT A PONY, #7: RUNAWAY PONY, #16: THE MISSING PONY PAL, SUPER SPECIAL #4: THE FOURTH PONY PAL, #6: TOO MANY PONIES, and #12: KEEP OUT PONY.

Other Pony Pal stories with Charlie Olson are #22: WESTERN PONY and #23: THE PONY AND THE BEAR.